THE
CHEETAH'S
TALE

STACEY INTERNATIONAL

London

THE CHEETAH'S TALE
published by
Stacey International
128 Kensington Church Street
London W8 4BH
Tel: 020 7221 7166 Fax: 020 7792 9288
E-mail: enquiries@stacey-international.co.uk
Website: www.stacey-international.co.uk

ISBN: 1 900988 879
CIP Data: A catalogue record for this book is available from the British Library

© Julia Johnson and Susan Keeble 2005
1 3 5 7 9 0 8 6 4 2

Design: Kitty Carruthers
Printing & Binding: SNP Leefung, China

The Cheetah's Tale

Written by Julia Johnson

Illustrated by Susan Keeble

For Alice and William,

and for Charlotte,

and with the author's thanks

to Ronel Smuts

for her technical guidance.

A conservationist footnote:

The buying of wild animals in the market place is not to be
encouraged, since this perpetuates the trade and leads to the
capture of cubs in the wild and to the killing of their mothers.

Foreword

It gives me particular delight to see *The Cheetah's Tale* in print. It is based on the true story of my own experience with a cheetah cub. It is thanks to the work of the Abu Dhabi Wildlife Centre and its staff that such stories can have a happy ending.

The Centre is a non-profit-making organisation working to ensure the continued survival of all endangered species, and is active worldwide gathering support and working with international and local conservationists, wildlife centres and zoos concerned with the conservation of the cheetah.

The Centre provides a sanctuary for orphaned and sick animals, and has an Education Centre where the public can learn about endangered species by observing them at close range, raising public awareness of the pressing need for wildlife preservation, particularly amongst the younger generation.

ADWC concerns itself with the breeding and management of several endangered wildlife species - particularly the cheetah in captivity. The ultimate objective of the Centre is to return these endangered African species to the wild when their numbers in captivity have increased to the point where they can successfully be rehabilitated and released.

This beautiful book will serve as a valuable tool in spreading the conservation message to the young - the conservationists of tomorrow.

Ronel Smuts
Director, Abu Dhabi Wildlife Centre

The Director of the Wildlife Centre with Nellie,
the cheetah on which this story is based.

Hidden among the branches of the fallen tree overlooking the water hole, she had a clear view across the wide African plain. The fierce heat of the day had given way to the cool of late afternoon, and the sun was an orange glow in the sky.

Apart from one small rabbit, she had not eaten for several days, and she could no longer ignore the pangs of hunger. But she must not be long! Cubs on their own were an invitation to jackals and other enemies. She had moved them to the safety of a new den only that morning, carrying each one gently in her jaws. She had left them sleeping soundly in the shade of the overhanging rock, their small forms hidden from prowling lions and leopards among the long grass. Soon they would be old enough to come with her, they would follow her waving white-tipped tail and she would teach them how to hunt.

She concentrated her gaze. With her keen sight she could make out the unmistakable white rumps of antelope in the distance. The herd was still a long way off but it was heading for the water hole, where giraffe and zebra were already gathered. She crouched lower in her hiding place.

Gradually the antelope edged nearer, their thirst driving them forward. Their ears twitched, their senses alert for any movement, any danger. But the cheetah was well hidden, her spotted body blending perfectly with the leaves and branches of the tree.

Stealthily she crept from her hiding place. Holding her head low she began to move towards the herd through the long dry grass, her eyes fixed on an antelope slightly apart from the rest, a young one, new to the game of chase. At that moment its mother sensed danger. The rest of the herd instantly picked up her signal, and began to run. This was the moment the cheetah had been waiting for. Her attention focused on her target, she leapt into action. Within seconds she was closing on her prey. But it was not to be that easy! The herd of antelope sprang in all directions. As

the young one veered to left and right, running and leaping after its mother, the cheetah followed each sharp turn without slowing down, using her long tail to keep her balance as she changed direction. The mother antelope turned, willing the youngster on.

Nothing could compete with the cheetah's speed, she almost seemed to be flying. She was rapidly gaining ground. But she was tiring fast, she could only keep up this pace for a short time. This was her first big chase since giving birth to her cubs. If she failed, she would go hungry again. With a final burst of speed she covered the space between them. A swipe of her front paw, and the little antelope was knocked off its feet. Pulling it to the ground with her big claw, the cheetah bit into the antelope's throat, and held on until it stopped moving.

She dragged her kill into the shade of some nearby bushes. Too soon the vultures would descend, a sure sign to hyenas that a meal was on offer. Unlike the cheetah, they were only too happy to steal another's dinner. Hurriedly she tore meat from the rump. Her hunger satisfied, she left the carcass for other scavengers. She did not notice the prying eyes of a jackal watching her. There would be easy pickings for his family this evening!

About half
way home she
stopped   and
pricked up her
ears, she could hear
an unfamiliar sound. She
melted into the long grasses as the
jeep sped over the rutted track, leaving a
cloud of dust in its wake. Hurrying on, she could
make out the overhanging rock in the distance now.
She was tired, she had used all her energy in the chase,
but she must get back to her cubs. They depended entirely
on her, there was no father to keep guard whilst she was away.
Already two out of her four cubs had been taken by a hyena.

Something stopped her in her tracks. She sniffed the air. A pungent odour filled her nostrils. The fur on her neck stood on end. Her chirping call carried on the still air, but there was no answering call.

In her hurry she did not notice the jagged piece of glass, but she did not have time to stop and lick her wound. A few bounds and she was at the rock. The grasses had been parted. Strange prints covered the ground. And the smell here was much stronger. Where the cubs should have been, only the warm imprint of their bodies remained.

For several days the mother cheetah returned to the rock. She searched the surrounding grassland for long hours. Her plaintive call echoed over the wide African plain. But there was no reply.

* * * * *

In the hold of the great wooden dhow the two small cubs huddled together for comfort. The ship rocked and rolled as it ploughed its way through the rough sea. The cubs were frightened. They wanted their mother. They wanted to drink her warm milk. They wanted her to wash them clean. They wanted to hear the soft safe sound of her purring. And more than anything else, they wanted her closeness.

They had not seen the blue of the sky or felt the warmth of the sun since the moment when those big hands had snatched them from their warm bed. Spitting and struggling, they had been dropped into a big wooden crate. The lid had come down with a bang, blocking out the daylight, and removing them forever from their mother, and from the safety of their small world, a world where one day they would have had the freedom of the great African plains.

Now they hardly had room to turn round. Even if they could, they no longer wanted to roll and tumble and play. The distinctive tear lines running from their eyes seemed to echo the sadness in their hearts.

And they were afraid! They were afraid of the darkness, of the creaks and groans of the dhow, of its terrible pitching and tossing, of the rotten lumps of stinking meat which were sometimes thrust between the bars of their cage and which they were too young to eat. And they were instinctively afraid of the snake which was coiled up in a glass box opposite them. At first they had been too terrified to notice anything, they huddled together and kept their eyes closed. The larger of the two had opened his eyes first. When the snake reared its head and its forked tongue darted in and out of its mouth, the cub bared his small teeth, his fur stood on end and he backed away in alarm. He knew that snakes were dangerous – it was the first lesson their mother had taught them, he remembered her warning chirp to keep away, as one had slithered through the long grass.

A small boy appeared. He looked at the cheetah cubs through the bars of their cramped prison, and they looked back at him. The boy knew that the little cubs had been trapped. "They do not belong here," he thought, "and neither do I." He too wanted his mother, he longed to feel her big plump arms around him and to hear her rich warm voice singing songs of home. But his family was poor, and he could earn money working on the dhow. He cleaned the decks and chopped food for the men. He had helped to stow the sacks of coffee and rice in the hold. He had seen the big crate being brought on board, but when he had asked what was inside he had been told to mind his own business.

The boy knew about poachers, his grandfather had told him. He knew that they caught young animals to sell; he knew that they killed elephants and sawed off their tusks. The wise man of his village said that the animal spirits would take their revenge, and he should know. Silently he prayed to the god of all things that one day these cubs would see the green plains of Africa again.

* * * * *

Sara loved the maze of winding alleys which made up the old bazaar. She and her mother often went treasure hunting, for you never knew what you might find there! She breathed in the scent of heady perfumes mingled with mysterious spices. An eye-catching display of colourful fabrics jostled for attention next to a towering stack of huge aluminium pots and pans. She lingered to watch the metalworker as he beat the hot copper into curious shapes. What was he making today, an enormous ladle perhaps? A coffee pot with a long spout? Old men sat and talked and smoked their hubbly bubbly pipes. Traders offered nuts and dried apricots as you passed. Gold bangles set with shining jewels glittered when they caught the light. And everyone wanted to show you something.

This morning Sara stopped as usual to gaze up at the little yellow canary singing his heart out in his tiny cage. She felt sorry for the little bird, she knew that he sang for want of a mate. He was lonely. The man who owned the shop suddenly appeared at her side. "Come," he said, "Follow me. I show you." She hesitated, not sure whether to follow him or not. "Come," he said again, "I show you cats." Then, seeing her uncertainty, he added, "Cats with spots." And he drew spots on his arms with a finger to show her what he meant.

Now Sara was only eight, and in her experience cats came in a variety of colours. She had seen black ones and white ones, her aunt owned a very snooty Siamese and her grandmother had kept an even grander Persian. She knew of tabby cats, and she had read a lovely story about a ginger tom. But she had never seen a spotted cat. Her curiosity got the better of her, and she followed the man into the back of his shop.

A bad smell filled her nostrils. It took a moment for her eyes to get used to the gloom. Then what she saw made her heart lurch. Two cats were huddled together in a cage barely large enough for them to move. They were sitting in their own filth, and their only food was a bowl of dirty water. She peered more closely. Sure enough the cats had spots just as the man had said. "See," and he waved his hands triumphantly, "cats with spots." Suddenly Sara realized what she was looking at. "Of course! How stupid of me!" she thought. They were not pet cats at all, but they did belong to the cat family.

The man mistook her silence. Thinking that she was unimpressed, he took a stick and jabbed the bigger of the two cubs. Instantly it snarled and hissed and spat like a wild thing – which, of course, it was! The man laughed delightedly, revealing large gaps between his teeth. He was taken by surprise when Sara snatched the stick from him. "No!" she cried angrily. "No, you mustn't do that," and then, realizing that he was offended, she added, "please." A thought came to her. "How much?" she asked, pointing at the cubs. He rubbed his chin and looked at her, "One? Two?" he asked. "Both of them," she said firmly.

Now the man knew that the cats were unusual, he had never seen any with spots before. But he also knew that they were in poor health, the smaller of the two looked particularly frail, and he did not know how to look after them. They would be worth nothing dead. It would be as well to sell them reasonably and get them off his hands. On the other hand here was an eager customer, he would be a fool to let them go too cheaply he reasoned. He named his price. Sara told him that she would come back, and she hurried out of the shop.

She found her mother a few doors away, fingering some silver beads. Fastening them around her neck, she turned to Sara. "What do you think?" she asked. "Do you like them?" She stopped when she saw Sara's face. "Mum, quick!" said Sara breathlessly, "Come with me." Sara's mother hastily took off the beads and followed her daughter. "What is it?" she asked, trying to keep up with her, "What's wrong?" But already Sara was leading her mother into the shop.

On seeing them, the man grinned. Good, she had come back, and brought her mother. Perhaps he would make a sale. He followed them through to the back of his shop. He pointed proudly to the cage, "Cats with spots," he said once again. Sara and her mother looked at each other.

"How much?" her mother asked. "These very special cats, very rare, very good," the man began. Sara's mother cut him short. "Not good. Not good at all!" she snapped, "Don't you know that it is against the law to trade in this sort of cat?" The man did not understand, he shrugged his shoulders helplessly. "Police," she said. "Close shop!" and she mimed the door being locked, and handcuffs being clapped on his wrists. At this he looked afraid. The price dropped.

Sara's mother paid him. The man called a boy to carry the cage to the lady's car. The boy looked alarmed, he was frightened of the cats. A grimy cloth was flung over the bars and the boy warily picked up the cage and staggered with it behind Sara and her mother.

In the car on the way home Sara said, "They're cheetahs, aren't they? At first I thought they might be leopards, but when I noticed their tear stripes I knew. Poor little things! How do you think they got here, Mum?" Her mother shook her head sadly. "Poachers, I'm afraid," she said, "and it happens all over the world."

At home Sara helped her mother to carry the cage round to the back of the house. She found the paddling pool by the shed, and they filled it with warm soapy water. "We don't want to make the little creatures any more nervous than they are already," said her mother, "but we can't leave them in that state." But when they uncovered the cage they found that it was already too late to help the smallest cheetah. Its tiny body lay unmoving, it was nothing but a bedraggled little bag of bones. Sara lifted the lifeless creature out of the cage, it lay in her lap, cold and stiff. Sara could not hold back her tears. Her mother gently took the dead cub from her and wrapped it in a cloth. Later they buried it together in the garden.

The remaining cub was stronger and it kicked and squirmed in its efforts to stay where it was. Sara and her mother put on thick gloves to protect themselves from scratches. Her mother held the little cub by the loose fur on its neck, and Sara sponged away the filth from its coat. "It's just a baby, isn't it?" said Sara. Her mother nodded. "Poor little scrap, I shouldn't think it's more than five or six weeks old. Look, it still has its silvery mane. It won't lose that until it's about two-and-a-half months old." They wrapped the wet little creature in a big towel. Once dry, the hair on its back and head fluffed up thickly. Sara stroked its fur. "What's the mane for?" she asked. "To hide him in the grasses to protect him and keep him safe," her mother replied. "Well," commented Sara, "it didn't do this one much good."

Over the next few days Sara and the little cheetah got to
know each other. Sara was naturally quiet and gentle, and
she knew that sudden noise and movement
would only alarm the cub. She sat by his pen
whispering softly to him, and wondering
what kind of a person would steal a baby
away from its mother. Didn't they know
that he should be rolling and tumbling
with his brothers and sisters in the
sunlight? Didn't they realise that he
needed regular meals and exercise
and sunshine to develop strong,
healthy bones, just like any child?

As she watched him tucking
into the bowl of dry cat food,
she knew that she wanted this
creature to be her friend more
than anything in the world.

That night her mother discovered them both curled up together, fast asleep, the young cheetah cub nestled into the crook of Sara's arm.

* * * *

For as long as Sara could remember animals had been a part of her life. In South Africa, where she had lived until she was seven, Sara could have been lonely without children of her own age near by to play with, but that had never mattered because the house had been full of animals. They had been her friends! She had hated leaving them. But now she had Flag! She had decided on Flag as a name for the little cheetah because of the way he waved his tail about.

She soon discovered that bringing up a baby cheetah was a rough and tumble affair. As he grew, Flag liked nothing better than to knock her down and climb all over her! Sara was small for her age, so it soon became an uneven contest.

Sara did not tell anyone about Flag, she kept him her secret. But a few weeks later Mr Gough, her teacher, asked everyone in the class to give a short talk about their favourite animal. Most of the children spoke about their pets. They brought in photographs of cats and dogs, hamsters, rabbits and goldfish, and horses.

By the time it was Sara's turn the children were becoming restless. She had never stood up in front of the class before, but she swallowed her shyness. "My favourite animal is," she began, and then she changed her mind. She wouldn't say that it was a cheetah, she would let them guess. She started again. "My favourite animal has gleaming golden eyes," and she went on to describe the cheetah's small head, his strong muscular shoulders and long legs. "A tall cat," one boy called out. Everybody laughed! But everyone was listening. Sara smiled too. She was enjoying herself!

For five minutes or more she had them guessing. When she told them that the animal was spotted, the class joker called out again. "A tall cat with measles," he said, but another voice called out, "A leopard." "A leopard's eyes are green," Sara said, "and his spots aren't round solid black spots. My favourite animal has a long tail ending in three black rings and a white tuft." Still they didn't guess. "Its feet are like running shoes, the claws are uncovered and work like spikes. It can run up to seventy miles an hour! In fact it's the fastest animal on four legs." That did it! "A cheetah!" shouted several children together.

Sarah told them about the African veld where Flag would have been born. She told them that cubs would never know their father because the male leaves after mating with the female. "How do you know so much about them?" asked Majeed, who prided himself on being top of the class and knowing more than anyone else. "I suppose because I come from South Africa," she answered. "My uncle is a game warden and he often asked my mum to take care of a sick animal for him." Then she added, "And I have a cheetah cub at home."

"Oh yeah!" shouted Majeed. "Don't be daft, cheetahs don't live in this country."

"It may surprise you to know," Mr Gough interrupted, "that cheetahs probably once lived in all sorts of places where you wouldn't expect to find them today. There are pictures of them in ancient Egyptian tombs. They were trained to work with man, to hunt with him, and they were faithful to their masters, just like dogs. In fact they are still used as watch dogs today in some parts of Egypt."

The bell rang, and it was time to go home. As Sara was leaving with her mother she heard Majeed say to another boy, "Teacher's pet, she makes things up," and she knew that he was talking about her.

Flag was in his pen when she got home. He was pacing up and down the length of the wire netting. "Just like an animal in a zoo," the thought occurred to Sara, but she quickly pushed it out of her mind. This wasn't a zoo, he had a lovely big grassy run and a tree to sit under when the sun got too hot. Anyway Flag was free most of the time, wasn't he? She unlocked the gate, and Flag bounded over. He leapt at her in delight! Sara lay on the grass laughing. Flag was growing fast and he didn't know his own strength. She pushed him away as he tried to lick her face. "Ouch!" she exclaimed, "your tongue is like sandpaper!"

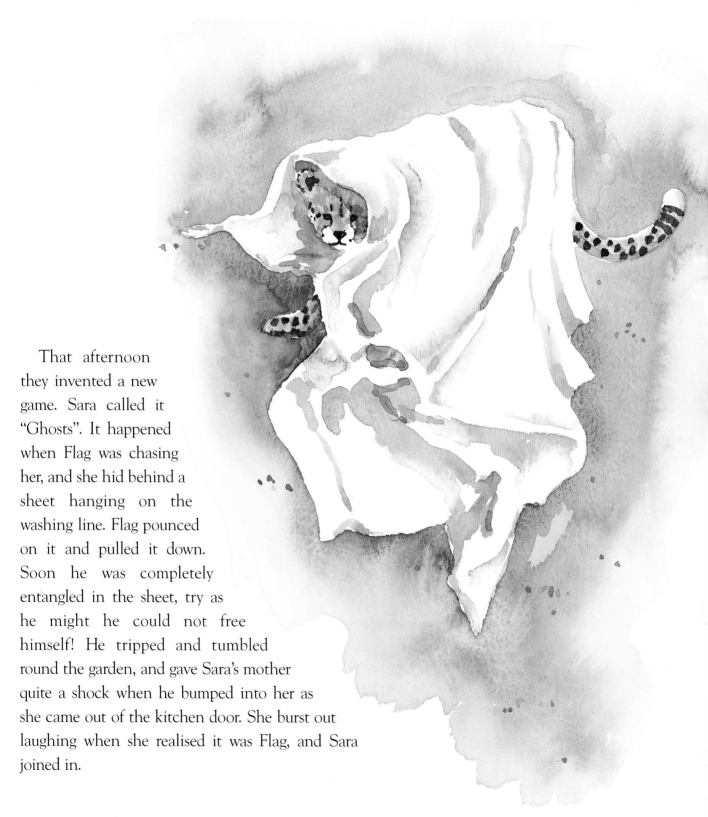

That afternoon they invented a new game. Sara called it "Ghosts". It happened when Flag was chasing her, and she hid behind a sheet hanging on the washing line. Flag pounced on it and pulled it down. Soon he was completely entangled in the sheet, try as he might he could not free himself! He tripped and tumbled round the garden, and gave Sara's mother quite a shock when he bumped into her as she came out of the kitchen door. She burst out laughing when she realised it was Flag, and Sara joined in.

Her mother noticed the change in Sara. She was no longer a quiet, shy little girl. Her mother was pleased, and she knew that it was all thanks to Flag.

One evening before she said goodnight, her mother sat down on Sara's bed. "Have you noticed how big Flag is getting?" she asked, "and he's lost his silver mane so he must be at least two-and-a-half months old now."

"He's already taller than I am," Sara said proudly. "If he were in the wild," her mother went on, "his mother would be teaching him how to hunt." "Well, he doesn't need to hunt with us," said Sara quickly, "we give him all he needs." Her mother looked troubled. "Do you think so?" she asked. "Yes!" Sara almost shouted it. "We give him food and shelter, he trusts us, and I love him more than ... more than ..." Sara's love for him was so great that she couldn't begin to measure it. Her mother smiled at her. "I know you do, but don't forget that cheetahs aren't pets, we can't keep him forever," she said, and kissed her goodnight.

Sara lay awake for a long time. At last she fell into a restless sleep. In her dreams she was once again in Africa. She saw the cloudless blue skies and the endless veld. On an anthill overlooking a water-hole sat a cheetah. Suddenly it moved, its form streaking like lightning across the plain until it was nothing but a blur.

She woke up with a start and sat bolt upright. She felt
hot and her forehead was damp.
    Could that cheetah be Flag?

At breakfast the next morning Sara looked miserable. "Have you forgotten that your class are coming to see Flag today?" her mother asked. Sara brightened.

Flag charmed them all, even Majeed. They wished that they could roll and tumble, and play chase and hide-and-seek with a cheetah, the way Sara did. It was wonderful to watch them together, they seemed to understand each other. Sara could imitate Flag's purrs and chirps, and even Majeed was secretly impressed.

The next day he came over to Sara in the playground. "Do you want a sweet?" He offered her the bag of jelly babies. Sara wondered if it might be a trick, but she took one anyway.

"Is it true about the father cheetah leaving the mother after…", he began, and blushed, "after…you know…?" Sara nodded. "My dad left," Majeed whispered, "after I was born." Then he added quite fiercely, "But don't you dare tell anyone." Sara shook her head, she wouldn't, though she wasn't sure why Majeed was confiding in her. They looked at each other. "It must be quite something to have a cheetah for a pet," Majeed said.

"You can come and see Flag again if you want to," Sara said. "Can I? Really?" Majeed asked eagerly, and Sara nodded.

She hadn't really expected him to come,

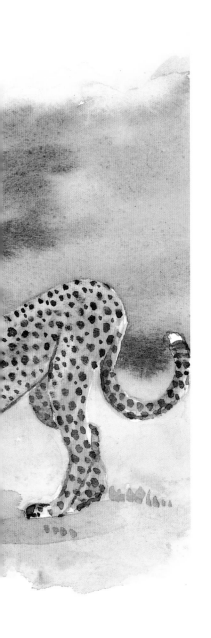

and so she was surprised when he turned up at the house the following afternoon. And after that Majeed came round most days.

Unlike Sara, he was not familiar with wildlife, and the cheetah fascinated him. He had so many questions! Sara told him how she and her mother had rescued the cub from the bazaar, and how they had nursed him back to health. "We had to give him lots of vitamins," she said, "and medicine to get rid of worms. He had to have injections as well, to protect him from diseases."

The cheetah quickly learnt to trust Majeed, and to expect his visits. Even before he was through the gate Flag would begin to chirp excitedly! As soon as Majeed joined in, their games became more boisterous than ever! Majeed loved to race through Flag's run, waving an old fur glove on a length of rope in front of the cheetah, making it jump about like a rabbit, and Flag would pounce upon it and shake it fiercely! Sometimes he would climb into the tree, his claws were still razor-sharp, and hide in the branches. Once he missed the glove when he leapt from his perch, and caught Majeed's leg and drew blood. Sara's mother dabbed the cut with disinfectant. "Flag is growing too big and too strong for these sort of games," she said.

One afternoon Majeed found Sara in tears. She quickly brushed them away when she saw him, but no matter how hard she tried to stop them the tears kept on coming. "What is it?" asked Majeed anxiously, "What's the matter?" He felt in his pocket for a tissue, but only found some screwed up sweet papers and a pebble. "Has something happened to Flag?" he asked, for he could think of nothing else which would upset Sara like this. She shook her head, and thrust the letter at him. It was from Sara's uncle, the game warden in South Africa.

When the letter had arrived her mother had given it to her to read. Sara had expected it and dreaded it, but she had managed to push the thought of it to the back of her mind in the hope that it would never come. She remembered running out of the house to find Flag. She had sat on the ground outside Flag's pen and looked at him. As usual Flag had bounded over and hurled himself against the wire, inviting Sara to come in and play with him.

But sensing Sara's mood, he had sat down. She had looked into his eyes, his wonderful glowing amber eyes. "Do you dream of Africa, Flag?" she had asked. "Is that where you belong?"

Majeed looked at the letter. "The rehabilitation programme is going well," he read, "and we have even had some success releasing cheetahs back into the wild. If Flag is healthy and fit enough to travel I suggest you organize the permits." Majeed looked up, "I don't understand," he said. Between sniffs and hiccups Sara explained. "It isn't right to keep Flag as a pet," she said, "and my uncle has agreed to take him at the centre. I suppose I always knew that we would have to take him back to Africa one day. Flag should be given the chance of freedom. It may not work," she finished, "but it's worth a try."

And so the decision was made: Sara and her mother would take Flag back to the land of his birth.

A box was made for him to travel in, and Sara put in his favourite toy and one of her sweaters so that he would feel safe. In the semi-darkness he slept through most of the long flight, but Sara was awake every second of the journey. Her uncle was waiting for them at the airport, and he drove them in his Land Rover to the reserve.

When Sara woke up the next morning she struggled for a moment trying to remember where she was. She looked out of the window. A hornbill was perched in the thorn tree, and beyond the fence she could see a family of warthogs hurrying after their mother's waving tail as she led them to the water hole. Zebra and rhino were already gathered there. They belonged here, here beneath the African sky. Flag belonged here too. She knew it in her heart. She knew that freedom was the greatest gift she could

give him. And she accepted that the greatest gift was often the hardest one to give.

"Come to the centre with me," her uncle suggested after breakfast. He took her by the hand. "We'll take good care of Flag here you know," he said. "After a time in quarantine we'll probably be able to introduce him

to other cheetahs. Like this one over here," and he took Sara to a pen where a female cheetah lay in the shade of a tree.

She got up as they approached. "What was the matter with her?" Sara asked. "She had a nasty cut," her uncle told her, "it had turned septic and was poisoning her system, but the antibiotics did the trick and now she's fit and well again. She's been here a few weeks. When she was brought in she'd obviously been suckling her cubs quite recently, but unfortunately we couldn't find any trace of them." Sara pointed to the empty pen next door. "That one is for Flag. I thought you'd like to see his new home," her uncle said. "And with luck we may be able to release him into a large game sanctuary one day," he added, "but we'll always keep an eye on him."

Sara watched as Flag was introduced to his new home. Scenting the air, his nostrils quivered. Something familiar and dimly remembered came back to him. Alone with him, she said her goodbyes. "I can't play with you any more," she told him, "and I can't stroke you, you won't make friends with other cheetahs if I do. But I'll always love you, Flag," and she buried her face in his fur one last time. He tilted his head on one side enquiringly and licked away her tears.

When Sara flew home she found a small package waiting for her. It was from Majeed. Inside it was a framed photograph. He had taken the picture himself the day the class had come to visit. It showed her standing with her arm round Flag's neck. She stood the picture on the table next to her bed. It was the last thing she looked at before she turned out the light. "Don't forget me Flag," she whispered into the dark.